MAKING PICTURES

by Kristin Cashore

Strategy Focus

As you read, **evaluate** which way of making pictures you like best.

 HOUGHTON MIFFLIN   BOSTON

Key Vocabulary

crayons colored wax used for drawing

chalk a tool for drawing and writing

copy to make a thing like another

powders very tiny pieces; dust-like

smock a kind of shirt worn over clothes

practice to do something many times

ruin to hurt or spoil something

Word Teaser

A cook wears an apron. An artist wears a _____.

Do you like to draw and make pictures?

Artists make pictures in many different
ways. Some artists use paint to make pictures.

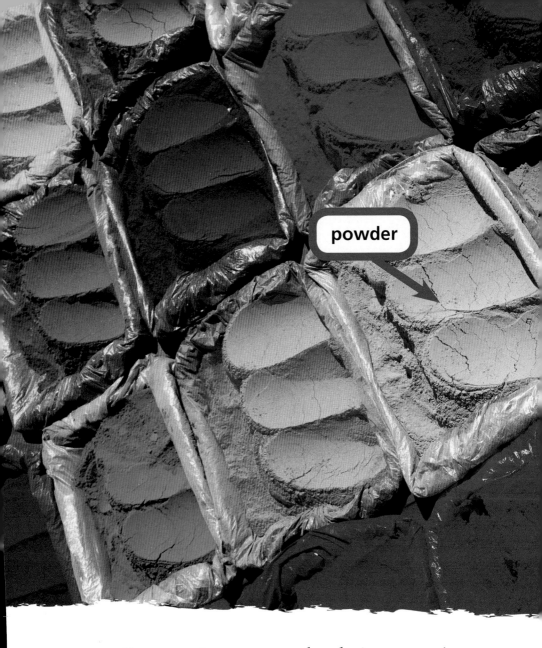

Some artists even make their own paint.
They mix colored powders with water or oil.

crayon

Some artists use pencils to draw pictures. Other artists draw with crayons.

6

Some artists use a special kind of chalk to draw pictures.

Now, are you ready to make a picture?
Do you want to copy one of the pictures in
this book?

Find a smock and a good place to work. Do not worry about making a mess. You can always start again if you ruin your picture.

There is one more thing to remember. To become a good artist, you need plenty of time to practice. Now get to work and have fun!